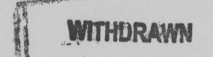

Time
for the
Fair

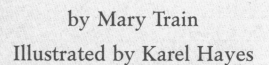

by Mary Train

Illustrated by Karel Hayes

Down East Books
Camden, Maine

Story copyright © 2005 by Mary Train

Illustrations copyright © 2005 by Karel Hayes

Printed in China by Jade Productions

5   4   3   2   1

ISBN 0-89272-694-6

Down East Books

Camden, Maine

a division of Down East Enterprise, Inc.

Book Orders: 800-766-1670

WWW.DOWNEASTBOOKS.COM

Library of Congress Control Number: 2005927184

The Farmer's Fair came once a year. Grace loved the Farmer's Fair.

She loved to see the animals and the big pumpkins.

She loved to ride on the Ferris wheel and eat candy apples.
Grace wished she could go to the fair every day.

She was thinking about it one night as she and Mama cuddled in Papa's big, cozy chair. They were watching snowflakes float softly down from the sky outside.

"Mama?" asked Grace quietly. "Will the fair be here soon?"

"No, Little One," said Mama. "It will be a long time before the fair is here."

"How long, Mama?"

"Long enough for us to watch the snow fall and have fun playing in it many times. When the snow melts it will be closer to the time of the fair."

So Grace played in the snow.
She built snowmen and caught snowflakes on her tongue.

She had fun going down the hill very fast on her sled.

After many, many days, the snow melted and Grace asked Mama, "Is it time for the fair?"

"No, Grace, it is still a long time until the fair comes to town."

"How much time?" Grace wondered.

"Enough time for us to watch the rain fall and the world come alive again. When the grass is green, it will be closer to the time of the fair."

So Grace splashed in the puddles and made mud pies.
She picked yellow daffodils when their tube petals sounded their arrival.

One day, Grace ran across the green grass to bring a fresh bouquet of tulips
to Mama and she asked, "Now, is it time for the fair?"

"The time for the fair is getting nearer every day, but we still need to wait."

"How near?" Grace asked.

"Near enough for us to plant seeds in the garden.
When the pumpkins grow it will be almost time for the fair."

So Grace worked with her trowel and made many holes in the earth.
She tucked seeds safely in the ground.
She watered the soil many times and watched the plants grow in the heat of the sun.

The vines grew very long. When the plants sprouted round green pumpkins, she ran to Mama. "Is it time for the fair?" she asked breathlessly.

"It is just about time for the fair, Grace," said Mama.

"Just about?" asked Grace.

"Yes, just about time," repeated Mama. "It is just about time for the world to change color." When the pumpkins change from green to orange, it will, finally, be time for the fair."

So Grace watched the leaves on the trees turn red, yellow, and orange. She noticed the air was getting cool. The school bus drove by to gather children one day and she saw that the pumpkins were orange in the garden.

"Mama, Mama!" Grace screamed excitedly. "Now is it time for the fair?"

"It is time to gather wood for the woodpile and harvest vegetables for canning," said Mama. "It is time to pick the pumpkins and, yes, Grace, it is time for the fair. You have been so patient."

Grace couldn't believe her ears. She helped Mama ready everything to take to the Farmer's Fair. She picked out her favorite pair of overalls and sneakers to wear.

The next day, Papa loaded the biggest pumpkin into the truck, then he and Mama and Grace went to the fair.

They visited all the animal barns. The sheep were getting haircuts.
The goats wore coats to keep them clean. Some cows had baby calves.

The horses pulled heavy loads in teams.
Grace ate candy apples and rode on the Ferris wheel three times!

Her pumpkin won first prize for its size and bright orange color.

Grace loved it all.

At the end of the day, Papa carried Grace into the house. She and Mama cozied up in Papa's chair.

"How did you like the fair, Little One?" Mama asked.

"It was great, Mama," Grace said quietly as her eyelids grew heavy with sleep.

"I'm glad," whispered Mama. "You waited a long time."

"How long?" asked Grace wearily.

"A whole year," said Mama. "Winter, spring, summer, and fall."

"A year is a long time," whispered Grace.

Mama sighed, "Yes it is, Little One, yes it is."

Grace smiled. "A long time," she said, and fell softly asleep.